BLAST OFF BOY AND BLORP

FIRST DAY ON A STRANGE NEW PLANET

NEW PET

THE BIG SCIENCE FAIR

Blast Off Boy missed all his friends and family on Earth, but, at the moment, the one he missed the most was his dog, Scooter. 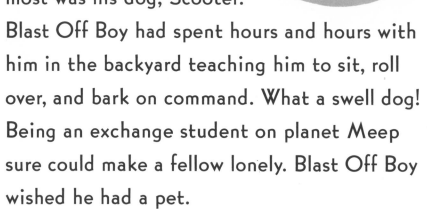 Blast Off Boy had spent hours and hours with him in the backyard teaching him to sit, roll over, and bark on command. What a swell dog! Being an exchange student on planet Meep sure could make a fellow lonely. Blast Off Boy wished he had a pet.

Blorp had never had a pet. Every Gloomp Day, Blorp would ask for a cute, cuddly schloppo, but his parents insisted he was too young and couldn't handle the responsibility. Maybe now that he was living on Earth with the Smiths, he'd be able to play with their dog, Scooter, and think of him as his very own pet.

That is, if Scooter ever came out from under the couch. . . .

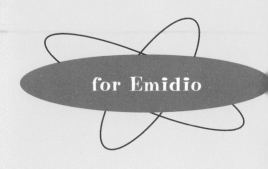

for Emidio

Text and illustrations copyright © 2001 by Dan Yaccarino

For information address Hyperion Books for Children,
114 Fifth Avenue, New York, New York 10011-5690.

First paperback edition, 2003

1 3 5 7 9 10 8 6 4 2

Printed in Singapore

Visit www.hyperionchildrensbooks.com

Library of Congress Cataloging-in-Publication Data on file

ISBN 0-7868-1429-2 (paperback)

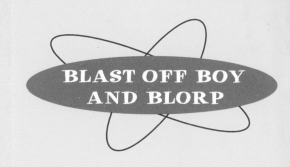

BLAST OFF BOY
AND BLORP

New Pet

written and illustrated by
DAN YACCARINO

Hyperion Paperbacks for Children
New York

Blast Off Boy woke up so early that there were only two suns in the sky. He opened his sleep pod and floated down to breakfast.

"Good morning, Blast Off Boy," Mrs. Glorp said as she served the family's breakfast capsules. "How many breakfast pills would you like this morning?"

"Only seventeen, please. I'm not that hungry."

Mr. Glorp burst into the room with Blippy, his daughter. "We have a big surprise for you!" he said happily.

"Hooray!" said Blippy. "A big surprise!"

Blast Off Boy was startled as a giant, slobbering green monster tackled him and stood on his chest, licking his face.

"W-what is this?" cried Blast Off Boy.

"Why, your new pet schloppo, of course!" Mr. Glorp laughed.

"I named him Twinkles," Blippy said.

"We thought you'd like a little pet," said Mr. Glorp.

The big green monster put Blast Off Boy's head in his mouth.

"Say, he's taken quite a liking to you!" said Mr. Glorp.

Then Twinkles chewed on Blast Off Boy's leg.
"Are you sure he's not trying to eat me?"
Blast Off Boy asked, covered in alien pet drool.
He wished he could have brought his dog,
Scooter, with him to outer space. Now, *there*
was a pet.

"**B**lorp, I think Scooter is still a little afraid of you," said Mr. Smith.

"He doesn't like new, uh, people," said Mrs. Smith. Blorp tried to coax the dog out from under the sofa, where he'd been since Blorp had arrived.

"Yes, Blorp," said Mr. Smith, "give him a little time to get used to you."

"The last time Scooter hid under the couch this long," said Lenny, "was the Fourth of July."

Blorp had never had a pet, and he wanted to play with Scooter something awful. This dog was no schloppo, of course, but he was still kind of cute.

"Very well," said Blorp, "I have to go to school, anyway. Come on, Lenny."

Later that day, on his way home from school, Blorp had a funny feeling that he was being followed. He turned around, and sure enough, he was.

A baby hippopotamus stood there smiling at him. Well, he *thought* it was smiling.

"Hello," Blorp said as he petted it. "Are you lost?"

The hippo blinked his eyes and swished his little tail.

"Would you like to come home with me, little fellow?"

The hippo's tail swished faster. Blorp was so excited. This could be his new pet! Then he remembered Scooter. Maybe Scooter would be afraid or even jealous of Blinky, as Blorp had decided to call the pet hippo. "I'll have to sneak you into the house," he told Blinky. "You'll have to hide in my room until I can figure out what to do." Blinky liked that and swished his tail some more.

Blast Off Boy decided to bring Twinkles to school for show-and-tell. He stood in front of the class with Twinkles on a leash. "Sit," Blast Off Boy said sternly to him. Twinkles licked Blast Off Boy's face. The class giggled.

"Ahem. Now, Twinkles, roll over," he commanded.

Twinkles sat up on his hind legs and drooled. The class laughed some more.

More embarrassed than ever, Blast Off Boy tried just one more time. "Speak!" he cried. Twinkles put Blast Off Boy's head in his mouth. All the children roared with laughter—except for Blast Off Boy.

"You sure have a funny pet," Blast Off Boy's friends Buzz and Bo said.

"Yeah," he replied, "real funny."

Blast Off Boy had never been so humiliated in his life. He scolded Twinkles and then tied his leash to the flagpole outside the school. Twinkles howled and cried, but Blast Off Boy ignored him. Blast Off Boy was *mad*.

Blorp quietly pushed
Blinky through the back door
of the Smiths' house and
guided him up the stairs to
his room. He was so happy to
finally have his own pet.

He tried to play catch with him, but Blinky ate the ball. He ate Blorp's pillow, his lamp, and then, his bed. Blorp thought that maybe his new pet was a little hungry. He fed Blinky all the food in the

kitchen, but he was still hungry. So Blorp fed him everything else in the kitchen—the table, the chairs, the oven, and even the kitchen sink. Then Blinky fell asleep.

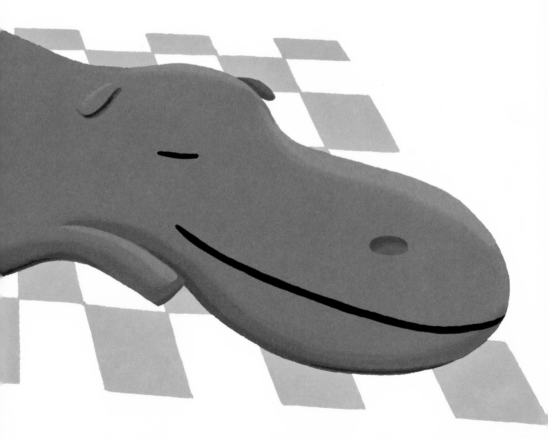

After school, Blast Off Boy spent the rest of the day trying to teach his new pet to fetch, roll over, and sit. When Blippy came home and saw this, she asked, "Why are you trying to teach Twinkles how to do these things?"

He didn't quite know why, but he knew what a good pet was supposed to do.

"Because," was the only answer he could come up with.

Unfortunately, Twinkles had no interest in learning how to fetch, roll over, or sit. He was too busy trying to lick Blast Off Boy's face or put his head in his mouth. Blast Off Boy still couldn't figure out if this meant Twinkles liked him or was just hungry.

The next day at school, Blorp pleaded with Mrs. Pomerantz to believe that his pet had eaten his chemistry homework. "Blorp, I know you're new here," she said, "but that is the oldest excuse on the planet."

Then, Blinky, who must've missed Blorp very much, burst into the classroom and ate everyone else's homework, too. Blorp petted Blinky, and Blinky wagged his little tail—he was happy to see Blorp.

"It's okay," Blorp called, "you don't have to be afraid of him. This is just my new pet, Blinky."

The class slowly peeked out from their hiding places under their desks.

"See?" said Blorp. "He won't bite you. He was just a little hungry, that's all."

The class petted Blinky's wide nose. He liked that very much. Mrs. Pomerantz told the class all about baby hippos: where they lived, what they liked to eat, what they liked to do, and how much they needed their mothers. She also told the class that she had read in the previous day's newspaper about a baby hippo that had escaped from the zoo.

"Maybe it was a different baby hippo," Blorp said to her, not wanting to give up his new pet.

"Well, Blorp," she said, "do you think Blinky would be happier living with you, eating your homework, or back in the zoo where he can be with his mother?"

Mrs. Pomerantz called the Smiths and the zoo officials while the class said their good-byes to Blinky the hippopotamus.

After school, Blorp went to the city zoo with the Smiths to visit Blinky.

There he was, happily splashing about with his family in the cool, green water. When Blinky saw Blorp, he blinked and swished his little tail. Blorp realized that his room was no place for a hippo. But that didn't make him miss Blinky any less.

"I think I know where everything in my kitchen went," said Mrs. Smith.

"See, Mom," said Lenny, "I told you it wasn't me."

When Blorp got home, he sat alone and thought
about how much he missed his big, gray friend.
Blorp was sad.

Scooter tentatively peeked out from under the
couch. Then he jumped up and licked Blorp's face.

That was it. Blast Off Boy couldn't stand it any longer. Twinkles's howling was keeping everyone awake. He went outside to shut him up.

"Boroooooh! Boroooooooh!" Twinkles howled.

The sound seemed familiar to Blast Off Boy. It was sort of like the sound that his dog, Scooter, made when he was sad.

Twinkles hollered sadly some more, but his eyes lit up when he saw Blast Off Boy, and he drooled happily.

"What is it, Twinkles? What's the matter?"
Blast Off Boy asked him.

The schloppo nuzzled up next to him, and Blast Off Boy gave him a little cuddle.

There they sat together, a boy and his schloppo, looking at the stars and moons. Okay, Blast Off Boy thought, so he can't fetch, roll over, or sit on command. But Twinkles is still a good pet, anyway.

He gave his pet another hug, and Twinkles gently put Blast Off Boy's head in his mouth.

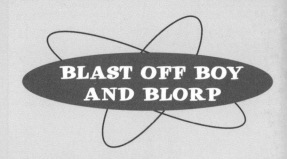

BLAST OFF BOY
AND BLORP

DON'T MISS
BLAST OFF BOY AND
BLORP'S ADVENTURES IN

THE BIG
SCIENCE FAIR

written and illustrated by
DAN YACCARINO

Hyperion Books for Children
New York

"**I** have some exciting news, class," Professor Plotz announced. "Our school is going to have a big science fair, and the best projects will get a prize!"

The class cheered. Well, everyone except Blast Off Boy, that is. He didn't think science was at all his best subject. But then, neither were advanced nuclear calculus, quantum chemistry, or galactic gym. And he wasn't too sure about recess, either.

On Earth, Lenny tried to keep up as Blorp raced home from school to tell the Smiths and their dog, Scooter, about the big science fair.

"There's a science fair at school," he excitedly told Mrs. Smith. "And I'm going to win first prize and get an award and have my picture in the newspaper and be on television and . . ."

"Now, calm down, Blorp," said Mrs. Smith. "Sit down and tell me all about it."

"I can't!" Blorp said excitedly. "I've got work to do!" So he raced upstairs to his room and let Lenny fill Mom in on the details.

For the rest of the day, Blorp stayed upstairs, planning out his brilliant, award-winning science project.

Dan Yaccarino is an award-winning artist and author who has created many books for children, as well as an animated television series for children, *Oswald*. He lives with his wife and children in New York City. Even without any four-legged friends, his home sometimes feels like a zoo.

The inspiration for the Blast Off Boy series came from Dan Yaccarino's experience of moving to a new home. Life in a strange new place was made easier for Dan by a string of dogs, cats, birds, hamsters, mice, fish, frogs, turtles, rabbits, snakes, and one chameleon, which hasn't been found since its escape in 1977.